CIVILIANS

CIVILIANS

POEMS

JEHANNE DUBROW

LOUISIANA STATE UNIVERSITY PRESS  BATON ROUGE

Published by Louisiana State University Press
lsupress.org

LSU Press Paperback Original

DESIGNER: Michelle A. Neustrom
TYPEFACE: Whitman

The book epigraph is from *Metamorphoses* by Ovid, translated by Charles Martin. Copyright © 2004 by Charles Martin. Used by permission of W. W. Norton & Company, Inc.

Cover image courtesy Abode Stock / neurobite.

LIBRARY OF CONGRESS CATALOGING-IN-PUBLICATION DATA
Names: Dubrow, Jehanne, author.
Title: Civilians : poems / Jehanne Dubrow.
Description: Baton Rouge : Louisiana State University Press, 2025.
Identifiers: LCCN 2024033322 (print) | LCCN 2024033323 (ebook) |
ISBN 978-0-8071-8372-4 (paperback) | ISBN 978-0-8071-8420-2 (epub) |
ISBN 978-0-8071-8421-9 (pdf)
Subjects: LCSH: Military spouses—Poetry. | LCGFT: Poetry.
Classification: LCC PS3604.U276 C58 2025 (print) | LCC PS3604.U276
(ebook) | DDC 811/.6—dc23/eng/20250719
LC record available at https://lccn.loc.gov/2024033322
LC ebook record available at https://lccn.loc.gov/2024033323

for Jeremy

My mind leads me to speak now of forms changed
into new bodies

—Ovid, *Metamorphoses*

CONTENTS

OPEN WATER

What Do You Give the War that Has Everything / 3
The Trojan Women / 5
Civilian / 6
Norfolk, VA / 7
Naval Reserve Officer Training Corps / 8
Hyacinthus / 9
When Diplomacy Married War / 10
The Billet / 11
My Husband's Father / 13
Brothers / 14
Apologia / 15
We Lived in Another Century of War / 16
Flight 2270 / 17
Civilian / 18
My Husband Learns of Another Sailor's Suicide / 19
Epic War Poem / 20
A War Is Forever / 21

OPENING INSIDE US

Metamorphoses / 25
i. / 25
ii. / 26
iii. / 27
iv. / 28
v. / 29
vi. / 30
vii. / 31
viii. / 32

ix. / 33
x. / 34
xi. / 35
xii. / 36
xiii. / 37
xiv. / 38
xv. / 39

OPEN SPACES

Some Final Notes on Odysseus / 43
The Veteran in a New Field / 45
Philoctetes / 46
The Acme No. 470 Clicker / 48
As You Were / 49
Civilian / 50
Hail and Farewell / 51
Open Spaces / 53
Trench Whistle / 54
Tyrian Purple / 55
Pygmalion and Galatea / 57
Rereading Ovid in Denton, TX / 58
As for Penelope— / 59
At the Poetry Conference, My Husband Is a Subject of Great Fascination / 61
Domestic Policy / 63
Pledge / 65
Civilian / 66

Acknowledgments / 67

OPEN WATER

What Do You Give the War That Has Everything

The first year, we were told, is always
the most difficult, a neutral zone
of afternoons and nights. Dear war,

we said, we are sending ourselves
folded inside gilded envelopes—
we have stamped your name in wax.

By the second year, we'd learned
to rip the bedsheets into strips
for bandages. This is the gift of cotton,

we said, that it soaks whatever seeps.
Soon there was leather. Soon there was
linen, the wood we burned

when supplies were cut to the front.
And later, there was iron melted
red and molded into spears,

the fruit shape of grenades.
In the seventh year, we gave
the war a heavy blanket made of wool.

Never mind, we said, the smell
of other bodies in the folds.
We forgot the year of bronze.

Year nine, we offered up
the decorative, a piece of pottery
painted with a chariot, a dead king

dragging through the dirt.
The war broke our present into shards.
After that, were years of tin and steel,

the tear of silk like a flag
the horses trample on, then lace
as with the tender bodice of a girl.

In the fourteenth year, there was ivory,
because why not pull down
the giants of the world. And next

a crystal cup for drinking victory,
a porcelain plate to serve
a traitor's head. In year twenty-five,

we engraved the war on silver.
This is costing us too much,
we said. We barely counted then,

the years of pearl and coral,
the ruby like a puncture wound,
the poison blue of sapphire set in gold.

The war took anything we had to give.
Decades on, we gave emeralds for
the green of some forgotten field.

We gave the war a diamond,
to honor its cleave and glittering,
its dreadful way of capturing the light.

The Trojan Women

We wore bright necklaces. We wore the dazzle
of a city. We were bodies draped in luxury,

the days ahead barely visible behind bolts of silk
that shimmered, gray to darker gray,

held this way, that way in the light.
Nothing was approaching from across the sea.

No thousand ships on the water and the water
barely rippling. We imagined the future

was a length of linen, the color of early morning,
or the yellow of uninterrupted sand.

And if a daughter saw what was coming,
her voice was birdsong we couldn't understand.

Of course, there was bad weather, a god
battering the walls with his furious rain.

There was sickness too—the madder-red
of some fevers, or the time honey went

mud-brown in the comb, the bees found dead.
But our beds were only a place of sleep,

not yet a funeral couch scented with saffron oil.
We were, ourselves, not yet divided.

Our necks were ringed with gold for years,
and why should we have questioned

how time would unroll in front of us, what snags
in the weaving, what quick unraveling.

Civilian

I bring the war into my bed each night
    and let it press metallic to my cheek.
I barely move beneath the trembling light
    that it emits, a semaphore both bright
and shadowy, its messages oblique.
    I bring a war into my bed. Each night
it floats across the sheets toward me—despite
    the little swells of fear, I never speak.
I barely move beneath the trembling light,
    the bite of sea salt on my lips, the slight,
unnerving sound of waves, the anchor's creak.
    I bring his war into my bed each night,
anticipate its sonar-ping, invite
    its touch. I know the heat its missiles seek.
I barely move. Beneath the trembling light,
    I am a target in the line of sight.
I am a shore toward which the cruisers streak.
    I bring our war into my bed each night
and barely move beneath its trembling light.

Norfolk, VA

In the early days, I visited his house,
slept beneath the flight path, the planes
that shook our bed with their landing.
It all needed work, but he was close
to the base, and besides, most of the time,
he would be on a ship somewhere else.
Later, he rented out the rooms to a guy
who never paid. And the family that left
feces on the floor, used syringes
like weeds growing from the carpet,
a curtain of cockroaches falling from the door.
The metaphor was too easy—
in his absence, he neglected home.
I didn't help with the cleanup.
It was enough to hear he returned
the house from its wildness,
the gloves he wore to touch the soiled story
of that place, the paper mask across his face.
The insects took months to leave,
resistant to all powders, sprays, their bodies
whispering, uncertain, heavy wings.

Naval Reserve Officer Training Corps

Lincoln, NE

Landlocked, the ship was a gymnasium
that smelled of students sprinting on the track,
the dust of cornfields in the distance.
Most afternoons, my husband drilled
cadets in the proper words for things—
that stairs were ladders. The walls,
called bulkheads, were painted gold and blue.
Schooner of the Plains, he liked to say.
And the wind was always blowing
on the lake, where classes tried to steer
their crafts by stars they couldn't see.
They practiced saying port and starboard.
They squatted in the grasses holding rubber rifles
in their sweat-wet hands. It was lazy work
to watch the students acting out a war,
fumbling in the bushes for a foe.
On Fridays, they wore uniforms,
felt the tightness of the collar. The cut
of khakis made it difficult to slouch
in their plastic chairs, my husband's voice
the low monotony of an engine running,
as if already they were on their first
deployment, a cruiser moving toward
the open water of a larger world.

Hyacinthus

Some afternoons I leaned into his arms,
the sheets rumpled in the way of carved marble,

or rested my fingers on the hard notch below
his throat, a place that also felt like stone.

It was simple, in that late light of the day,
to see something sculptural in us. I thought

of the god who lost his lover and wept—
oh, to be human, unenduring, to be a body

not forever beautiful. After the prince died,
Apollo made a flower from the blood,

a purple wound and its petals marked *alas alas.*
And lying in our bed, I could hear already, yes,

how I would tell this story. I would say
we held the scent of wet, green leaves.

I would ask whose hands had plucked the lyre.
In the myth, love was a metal ring that split the sky.

And couldn't I make a cluster of blossoms
from whatever hurt we left on one another?

Couldn't I chisel our faces out of rock?
From these little arts, we would go on and on.

When Diplomacy Married War

I was posted to partitioned cities,
to countries split by the long invasion
of history. I was trained to be tactful,
even toward the tanks, touched
my fingers to their protruding noses,
as is the custom in such places.
Perhaps, it's surprising I found
romance then, war marching
to the gates of the embassy.
It sat at the endless table
in the gilded room of negotiation.
War had big shoulders and barely
fit the crushed suit it wore. But, still,
I admired the drumming of its voice.
Its mind had an asymmetric beauty,
sea-blue and crisp in its skill
at flattening a town with the clustered
munitions of its thoughts.
Now we are married. And I concede—
I keep attempting a détente between us.
I offer caviar as an overture of peace,
slugs of vodka. I argue for
a wheat field left alone.
Don't trample through the barley,
I tell my war. Often, we agree
on nothing but the bedroom,
our zone of safe passage. If only
I could persuade it to foxhole
in the blankets, to nuzzle in the rubble.
If only I could stroke it into sleep.

The Billet

ten hours as the crow
          flies and yet some days

we're more than skies
                    apart   I hear the planes

landing they shake
          the deck in every call

their metal screech
                    as if to say it's not

enough that voices wing
          from ship to home

                    as if to say a marriage
made of distance

is always circling and still
          is not a feathered thing

~

          it could be worse he says
he could be underneath

the waves   he could be
                    held inside an armored

          body made for war
elusive fish

                    that only surfaces
in quiet months

the shore a glistening net
        to be evaded   and I

                could be waiting like a widow
who looks for any glint

a silver flicker
        in the unspeaking night

~

                ship-to-shore means
we speak rapidly as water

the line a length of rope
        pulled close to snapping

today I'm telling him
                        a week of words

                I pour an ocean
into the plastic ear of the phone

we try deciding everything
        between the ring   the

                click of disconnect
we call marriage a stone

it skips across the ragged
                        surface of the sea

My Husband's Father

has been walking away from the war
for fifty years, making a path through
the mountains to find an open air.
Up there, the firs resemble nothing
but themselves. There's no destruction
but the brush bent underneath his boot.
No one calls out except the hawk.
It's hard with his unaccustomed hands
to grasp at feelings, hold sadness
like a rough, misshapen cup.
He's taking a course in miracles.
He's trying to believe shadows are not
a bruise across the face of night.
For the past few months, his heart keeps
stopping, and he drops into the dirt.
At such altitude, memory is distant,
a country he visits in the breath
before waking to the spongy touch
of moss and a voice asking,
sir, are you okay, are you okay—

Brothers

Grown now, they have a way of getting close
that looks like combat, just as they used to
wrestle in the dirt or push each other from a bed.
Once, my husband enlisted. And his brother—
who studied the colliding physics of the stars,
distant explosions—refused to use his science
in the work of war. He marched to a nearby base.
He wore a slogan and carried a sign. With brothers,
it's a matter of fingernails dug in the tenderness of skin.
It takes knowing which bones were broken years ago.
Don't protest the soldiers, my husband said,
but the ones who send them off to fight.
Now the two are so far apart only something
droning very high could locate their coordinates.
One would need an instrument positioned
in the desert and pointing its curved mirrors
at the night, to track the light that they're emitting,
each keen certainty set against the other.

Apologia

It is hard to explain my love
for someone who fixes the engines
of invasion. Distance is critical,
a wide water of detachment,
first to caress his face and then
to describe the heart's neutrality.
I admit the heart should pick a side.
It should not adore an officer
whose job is to operate a system
named for a shield of Greek mythology,
releasing from the ship a missile—
a word that means capable
of being thrown, a thing that's sent,
like missive, as in a letter
sent to the cherished overseas.
I admit the heart refuses to apologize.
It loves a man who serves the war.
It loves a man who cannot camouflage
all the terrains inside himself
made dangerous. What to do
with the apolitical heart,
so often indifferent to the grim
detonations that go off somewhere
faraway, that it should long
for the thundering and awe?

We Lived in Another Century of War

after Muriel Rukeyser

Sometimes we stirred one another
with our fingers, as if desire might be
instant coffee spooned into a cup,
weak but still the tannins like a pelt
on the tongue. Sometimes we tapped
messages on the glassy faces of devices.
it's fine, we said, it's fine. Sometimes
the front page filled its allotment of blood.
Sometimes the page was poppies,
a red field where we napped for weeks—
oh! asleep among the furred stems,
leaves hairy as a young man's legs.
Sometimes all we could touch were branches
pointing at a sky we couldn't read,
its gray like newsprint paper smeared
by rain. We stood at the window sometimes,
our seeing etched in lines, our noses
stubbed like rifles and lifting toward
the blindfolded birches up ahead.

Flight 2270

Before we take off for Tampa,
the pilot tells us over the speaker,

his voice like something sealed in a can,
to express our thanks to the military

and their families on the plane.
Obedient, the passengers applaud,

a few moments of sound
in the aluminum tube of our journeying.

I can't decide if I'm sitting still
to receive their gratitude,

having married a uniform years ago,
having pinned ribbons to the hull

of my husband's chest, having placed my ear
against the thrumming engine

of his heart, or if I'm trying to unhear—
they're not so much clapping

as brushing the war, its fine,
metallic shards from their hands.

Civilian

There's a ship inside my husband
that's full of passageways with shifting lights.
It floats most days across a flattened sea.

If only I could stand in each compartment,
touch the little place he falls asleep.
But this isn't a tour offered to civilians

while the vessel sits in port, and all the sailors
go out drinking for the night.
I haven't been able to follow him—

he walks the engine room,
the rumbling center of the self,
which is always on the edge of burning up.

Here little is fireproof. And I've failed
to learn the name for such distances
as between the shore and where he's going.

There are gray corners I can't know.
I say nautical miles. I say knots.
I say mist drifting over the steely surfaces.

My Husband Learns of Another Sailor's Suicide

Because this story isn't mine
to tell, I'll watch him through the window,
standing on the back porch in the rain,
the phone a coffined shadow
at his ear, and the fence a line
made jagged with what it's trying to contain.

Epic War Poem

What else but a soldier raging
by his shield. What else but the dutiful.
What else but a battle muralled on a wall,
and Troy a piece of artifice to gaze upon.
What else but the voice a garment
shredded in its grief. What else but ash.
What else but men on wooden ships for centuries.
Their keening is an arrow to the throat.
What else but kings. What else but the trebuchet
of years. What else but sawbuck fences
leaning near a field. What else but America.
What else but daguerreotypes, a line of corpses
posed within the frame. What else but the guns.
What else but the trenches stuck with mud.
What else but modernity and the long
parade of after. What else but cinders
mixed with milk while the scorched are drifting,
processed into smoke. What else but the skirmishes
of scholars, language too little and too much.
What else but brief eras of indifference
when the dead are left alone. What else
but the forged and hammered thing
of poetry, all the failures of our making.
What else but the litany of bombs.

A War Is Forever

When picking out the perfect war,
we considered weight, its clarity and cut,
the color of its smoke above the city.
We looked for flaws and bruises.
To test for hardness, we dragged
the edge of war across a piece of glass.
The best wars, we knew, were brilliant—
a scintillation of the eye, their flash
a rainbowed fire. We wanted a war
so large it left an absence in the earth,
the kind of beauty that meant blood.
We kneeled in the mud of our passions.
Darling, we said to the shine of war,
nothing is more dazzling than your love.

OPENING INSIDE US

Metamorphoses

i.

It's the old story of division,
some god undoing the earth
from the sea, as Ovid says,

arranging the world into light
and denser elements.
I might give my husband

an ancient name. I might say
he is part divine, only his heel
omitted from the water,

this liquid narrative of a man
who is, for a time, one thing,
and then when the ocean

withdraws from land,
he becomes a new kingdom
in conflict with himself.

ii.

Or more to the point,
I am speaking of the uniform
stripped from a body.

For good, my husband says,
by which he means his armor
has been buried in the sand.

iii.

Perhaps he is now like the hero.
Observing Diana bathing
at the stream, the blue-veined

shimmer along her breasts,
he feels the sudden fur
on his skin and the antlers

soft in their velvet.
Peacetime is an unforgiving
goddess. She tears anyone

who looks too closely,
stepping from the pool
to the rocks' serrated edge.

iv.

Or if, like a curved mirror,
I turn the poem toward
myself, I am stilled to stone,

the snakes in my hair
unhissing, each tiny mouth
forever fanged and open.

v.

Always there's a chase.
Someone flees the arrows
of desire, longing a weapon,

no matter what I call it,
a metal jab in the heart.
The body will do anything

not to be taken—this time,
it melts into water.
I'm saying my husband

dodges the names I aim at him.
He becomes a stream,
slipping through my hands.

vi.

Do not offend the gods.
For weaving these scenes
on an upright frame,

I am withered to the size
of a dried seed, curled
spider in the corner.

Pallas has torn my tapestry.
No one will see my husband
weft-held in the loom—

once, I rendered his uniform
a twilight blue, starshine
of buttons down his chest.

vii.

At this point in the poem,
some king declares war,
and the city grows

a forest of bristling spears.
Even the soldier turned
civilian feels

for the iron edge,
which is to say, he feels

for the blade his body was.

viii.

Tonight, I shadow him,

or the story I've made

of him, around sharp bends,

the labyrinth a sentence

running on, and one of us

is a monster kept alone,

half human, half a thing

of horn and hunger,

and the other built these walls,

and we're tangled both

in trying to get out, the thread

we follow with our fingers.

ix.

People keep changing from fins
to dapple-hide to flicker-tail.
They slip into new skins.

x.

And here's the familiar story
about looking back. At the edge
of the underworld,

the singer sees only
a wisp of the beloved

before her body disappears.

So too with my husband.
I'm listening for his footfalls
behind me in the fog.

If I turn to see him following,

he's already leaving
in a slender twist of smoke.

xi.

Here's another lesson: it's best
to leave what I love alone,
or risk the husband gone

to gold. First his feet harden.
Then the shine travels his legs,
all of him gleaming,

gilt at his mouth and eyes.
Until soon he is precious
and metal to my touch.

xii.

Sometimes a hero dies
and later is burned—his ashes

barely fill a modest urn.

More often the soldier
simply stops being one.
His sword-arm aches

at the cold or rain.
His vision narrows inside
the memory of the helmet

he no longer wears,
the battleground barely a slit.
More often, what's left

of his voice goes rough,
as though scraped with a blade
or dragged over stones,

as though a bird rubbing
its feathers in the dust
to clean away dried blood.

xiii.

After the fighting stops,
grief is like a god
changing us into something else.

Our weeping grows fur,
a tail curved like a knife.
We howl at the gate, dogged

and scratching to get in,
how our grief wants to eat,
wants to sleep on a velvet bed.

xiv.

And now even the bodies
of warships lose their shape.
Ropes are ripped apart,

hulls pushed under,
the skins of vessels made skin,
cerulean in the waves.

The sailor is forced to stay
on land. The horizon doesn't change—
for weeks it's fixed and flat,

no god swirling the journey,
the days no longer ruled
by the water's changing mood.

XV.

What then? My husband
sleeps on his side and doesn't wake
to rummage in the gray light

for his uniform. He is altered.
And I keep trying to make a poem.
Sometimes we change

to stars or spotted lizards,
to pines, to trees without names.
We are turned into islands

or mountaintops. We are turned
to flowers that push through dirt.
We are sprigs of mint.

We are swans. We are owls
demanding answers of the dark.
We are flint struck against rock.

We are every kind of water,
still pond and stream opening inside us. We are small
currents searching for the sea.

OPEN SPACES

Some Final Notes on Odysseus

When the goddess cries out
to the Ithacans in Book 24,
her voice is a mountain against
the fighting. But the old soldier
keeps running—war like weather
in his ears, a summer storm.
At such a time it is difficult to see
Odysseus was a child once.
He learned from his father
the names of trees, the orchard
full of gleaming suns called apples,
the private ripeness of figs, grapes
clustered like families on the vine.
He touched their dusty skins.
Yes, even he had been a boy,
and he held a wooden sword.
There are decades of water,
islands and islands between
that child and the man.
The body is said to harden,
the heart of course as well.
For someone like Odysseus
anger is an unrestricted flame.
When the goddess cries out
she is saying, worship reason
instead. But it takes her own father—
a god and his thunderbolt
—to cut through the battle.
Stop this war, he says.
According to the story, Odysseus
lays down his weapons then.
And what then? What then?
Poems always end before the peace,
the orchard overgrown now.
No one wants to read a scene

of the old soldier pulling weeds,
pruning the wildness back, his arms
still strong but not with violence,
and the air no longer stings
like lightning touching down.
No one wants the old soldier
slicing a plum, just as he used to take
his dagger to the belly of a rival,
the war that fed him once a taste
he barely can recall. Most nights
his chin is red and syrupy with juice.

The Veteran in a New Field

Winslow Homer, 1865, oil on canvas

Already, he has worked like this for hours,
moving his scythe beneath the gold horizon.

There's stillness here. There is the swirl
of wheat, both what's been cut and what remains

standing, and the blade not so different
from a bayonet, a useful edge that's made of steel—

although it's best to forget everything
except the green and yellow glimmering,

brushstrokes of orange deeper in the field.
What little speckling of red there is, is at the root.

Mostly there's sky, a shade of blue
that might be called his child's eyes, or the blue

of a broken shell he once found tumbled from a nest.
There's the sweat that leaves a shadow

on his shirt and his uniform coat thrown far
to the corner of the frame and the shape

of his old canteen. Later, he will lift the dark
metal to his mouth and drink, until he barely tastes

the dust. He'll keep his gaze directed at the dirt,
behind him, the labors of the day laid flat,

and the grain giving way before him, falling
no heavier than light against the ground.

Philoctetes

I started with his mutilated arch.
And why not. The war was too large
a scene to paint on pottery, an amphora
crowded with chariots and spears,
anonymous figures and the red-clay sky
and even the ground clay-red.
When the snake attacked the soldier,
its fangs left a violent opening.
This I could render on ceramic,
his foot like a piece of fruit,
too ripe, the flesh gone purple.
And soon, the stink of rotting
everywhere. The other men couldn't sleep.
His toes, like dark grapes,
made their own bodies hurt.
Everyone forgot where they left the hero,
the sound of him calling
from the island's edge, and the ship's wake
like a small incision healing shut.
He waited ten years. This too I could paint—
the soldier limping over stones,
his foot now seeping, almost pulp.
There were other scenes I painted
in that time. His suffering had a shape
well-suited to a long-necked vase,
its terracotta mouth a grieving O.
Later, the men returned to take his weapons.
That's how the fighting would be won,
a wooden horse intestined full of men
and a city falling on itself. Combat,
they promised, could heal his wounds.
Arrows dipped in the juice of poison-
berries would cure him. Perhaps
they weren't wrong. Perhaps the war
could close the punctures of a serpent's bite,

like the cuts a potter makes, glaze
washing across the surface to leave behind
a faint and lustrous scar. And I keep
painting a study of his foot,
his ankle slender in the sandal-strap,
though nothing of what's underneath,
the war, a steady pulsing in his heel.

The Acme No. 470 Clicker

Signaling device carried by paratroopers in the 101st Airborne Division. D-Day, June 6, 1944.

The tool was pocket-sized, designed to rest
between a soldier's fingers and his thumb.
A toy. But when the metal was compressed
against the brass, it made the voice of some
lost insect in the dark. He clicked it once
to ask, are you an enemy or friend,
so brief the sound was barely utterance.
He listened for a clicking back. To spend
the night crouched in uncertainty, the rush
across the shadows, hours of pushing past
long grass—it's hard imagining the hush,
and then the stridulation, low and fast,
that, for a moment, quieted his doubt,
the little noise of crickets chirping out.

As You Were

To be a knot untied, a bowline cut,
a sheepshank slithered from its shape.

To be unpolished brass, a deck
unmopped, a porthole fogging

with the weather. To be unstriped
at the shoulder. To be a hand without

salute, a body left in its unease.
To be unmustering, unstanding

at attention. To be not as you were
for years. To be not hole or pit, not

maintenance, not snipe in coveralls,
unstained with engine grease. To be no

angle of attack. To be a missile aiming
nowhere but itself. To be sonar

pinging nothing, signal-jammed.
To be unwatered brown or blue.

To be breath unheld, unfloating
in the sea. To be both naught and not,

voyage without orders, no port of call.
To be unmapped, uncompassed,

points unfixed, no stars to navigate,
and all the sky unglittering and blank.

Civilian

For decades, I carried a plastic card,
    the word DEPENDENT at the top
and a small impression of my face below,
    dependere, meaning hanging down,
a weight. According to my husband,
    there used to be a way of finding
how far down the water went:
    a piece of lead fixed to a rope
was dropped over the side, the sailor
    counting the marked fathoms
until the burden touched the seabed.
    As for me, I was dependent
on his return. I weighted the end of his line.
    I measured the depth between us.

Hail and Farewell

> Atque in perpetuum, frāter, avē atque valē.
> —Catullus

When it's over, he wants to leave
without glasses raised together

at his going, no last salute or *sir.*
I admit to gratitude.

I've never stood at ease in the uniform
stillness of those wives,

dependents as they're known,
the watered silk of their voices

at a ball, or the brides who bend
beneath an arch of sabers.

Although I understand the day
must be lowered ceremoniously

received into our hands. I understand
we fold these endings

with neat and pointed corners.
Some parties welcome

new arrivals to command.
Some parties are for parting—

they take their names from poems
of the dead. I'm glad he takes

nothing with him when it's over,
not the flowers, not the picture

of a little ship, how it floats forever
in the matte-black frame of war.

Open Spaces

Now he is driving West Texas,
the dusty vastness not that different
from the oceans he used to watch
on the deck of a ship. For years,
that was his view and mine
in my imagining. The water
was like what I knew of him,
by which I mean a reflecting surface,
too dark to dive into. Outside
Marfa, he sleeps in a room
covered with dead moths,
their gray shadows everywhere
he touches, their wings
powdering his hands with failure
to take flight. He brings them
home in his suitcase, dead insects
in the creases of his clothes,
the way he used to bring me
a tiny jar of paprika, a tin of matcha,
a vial of crushed roses, souvenirs
to remember where he'd been.
Our open spaces are large enough
to hold all kinds of absence.
We trade one distance for another.
The wind keeps pushing across
whatever place he occupies—it leaves
small furrows on the land and sea.

Trench Whistle

I call my dogs with it, a blast of sound
that summons them from far across the grass,
and they come running at the trill, each hound
a blur of lead-gray fur, a yipping mass.
They only know the pleasures of the lawn,
the clovered fragrances. This cry I make
is like a strident bird that's quickly gone,
the branch now bare, the air that seems to shake
with what was there before. They can't conceive:
this whistle mobilized whole companies
of men. Its voice was sharp enough to cleave
the clamor of the front, the batteries
of mortar rounds. I call, and each dog runs,
unhunted by the terror of the guns.

Tyrian Purple

Please, understand: to heave Hector
through the dirt, Achilles must first
cut holes in his enemy's heels,
Hector threaded like a needle
with leather cord and tied to a chariot
that will pull him around the walls.
Imagine a body strong enough
to be strung like this. Imagine such
stitching is an art, and we call it battle.
Andromache deep in the palace
is weaving a cloak on a wide loom,
wool like the amethyst shadows
beneath her eyes, that vivid sleeplessness.
She's tacking flowers to the fabric
when she hears the weeping everywhere in Troy.
The bobbin unspools from her fingers
because the warp is a place of order,
and death the cutting shears.
Who can blame Andromache
if she sits at the loom for hours,
rectangular world where nothing extends
beyond the cloth's perimeter.
At this point in the war, everyone has lost
the thread of narrative, any reason
past armor and the carrion birds
with their beaks like sharpened secateurs.
Who wouldn't want to take up some craft,
pottery, perhaps, or painted scenes
on funerary stones. Don't hands need
occupation when the city is besieged.
Probably, a reader believes it frivolous—
these fibers dyed the plum of galaxies,
all that great, oppressive sky
and the murdered looking down
from their fixed constellations.

Even a wife must find a pastime.
It's late in our history to condemn
the ways people spin out a war,
if they twist the days like fibers on a spindle.
Imperial purple. Purple of bruised
loyalties. Unfadable purple
that stains the maker's skin.

Pygmalion and Galatea

You could say that, for decades,
I have carved him into life,
first heat overtaking the ivory
chill of his torso, then the rest,
down to his bruised arches.
I am like the sculptor who loves
the chisel's edge and the hammer
that splits a tusk in two—any tool
that requires inquisitive hands.
I keep chipping away to find his body.
According to the old story,
I should be naked on the plinth,
bent slightly back to accept
the artist's kiss. But I prefer reversals.
In this version of the myth,
I etch his face with a beard
and a tired groove in his forehead.
I add a map of scars to his palm.
No doubt it's easier to lift the mallet
than to be the one hewn from bone.
There is the knock of being seen.
Another's gaze can split
the self like a wedge. You could say
we're both a little weary now.
He's ready to climb down
from the pedestal, recover feeling
in his legs. And I have breathed
the scattered dust of him for years.

Rereading Ovid in Denton, TX

That verse can be confused
with foreign policy, all the intricate
mistakes a country makes—
this, Ovid understood.
Rumor has it desire banished him
past the edge of empire.
His exile was vermillion ink.
Carmen et error, he wrote,
the sea beyond Tomis dark as soot
or atramentum spilled across a page.
In those years, he wandered through basilicas,
the ground a mosaic of cut stone.
And what did he find in the patterns there?
—inlaid repetitions of the heart
wanting what it wants.
When a writer lives in furious times
pleasure can send him
to a distant shard of the world.
Although some say he was expelled
for other reasons, the tyranny
of the reader perhaps,
politics like a marble weight
on the curled corner of papyrus.
Poet, I return to you in a state
of rising heat where the scarlet sage
has its petals torn by wind.
Teach me to say small things
about union, the touch
of someone I love nothing more
than a quill tipped in red ochre.

As for Penelope—

after her husband reveals himself,
the divine costume dropping away
like rocks that tumble from a hillside,
she finds his face is a rough slab
but still familiar to the touch.
That first evening, intimacy is easy.
The couple remembers the way
to their bed. A goddess delays
the ending of night for hours,
the whole island held unmoving
so that the reunion stretches
like a lush vine over a wall.
We know this moment. We read it
together when we were twenty,
as far from our younger selves now
as a king trying to return to Ithaca.
At this point in the story,
most of the suitors are dead,
her husband having bent back
the bow as though it were a body
arched in pleasure. It's simple for us
to make metaphors that tie murder
to desire. The gasp of the dying.
The penetrative spear. The land too
loses itself in similes of conquest.
Like a lover to be claimed. Like
a beautiful woman asleep in shadow.
Later is more difficult to picture,
at least for me: she cleans the hall
of clotted blood, the piled
corpses pale as marble,
like ancient, unlimbed sculptures.
We say visceral to mean feelings
twisted deep inside the gut, grief
or anger sharp as a swallowed pebble.

We say commitment to mean
marriage is a rope we're tangled in.
Some days I think about untying it.
Where does the longing travel
when her husband sits close to her
at dinner, his fingers choked
around the hammered stem of a goblet.
What a boulder he has become,
all that history precarious,
the unsupportable weight of his love.

At the Poetry Conference, My Husband Is a Subject of Great Fascination

He leans at the back of the room,
holding my purse by its ink-black
straps, the leather limp, a creased
burden I have asked him to hold
while I answer questions
a few feet away. His legs slant
as if to indicate a linebreak,
that place where the sentence chatters on.
His forearms are scribbled
with words from one of my books.
And underneath his shirt:
more inked calligraphies.
The other poets want to touch a wrist—
how solid he is. *It's like I know you*
from her poetry, they say. This near,
they must smell the fragrance
on his neck, something of sea salt
and the evening washing in.
Last night, he stood with me, both of us
in our towels on the hotel balcony,
and watched a brown dog run past
a woman who tried to catch him
at the shore, his fur like a drift
of seaweed and the waves reaching
to his chest. And when, at last,
she held the dog and tethered him,
the leash a taut line, he sloped
all his weight toward the green
surface, ocean-froth on his face.
At the conference, the other poets
ask what my husband is doing now.
Thank you, they say, *for your service*.
Once, his horizon was water
and the ship a floating home. Now,

his work is to climb a wind turbine
to the top. The steel tower takes in
the sound of his boots, all breath
and fumble contained by the tunnel,
and higher above that, three blades,
and a view that continues for miles,
nothing but red dirt and mesquite,
feathered branch and thorn.
There are lives that turn inside
other lives. There are poems
that feel like standing close enough
to touch the man in the navy-
blue shirt, his eyes almost visible
beneath the curving line of a cap.
I know you, the others say to him.
I almost know you. Last night,
on the sand below our balcony,
the beach was white with shells,
most crushed or split imperfectly in two.
If you were to take off your shoes
and approach the pink scrawl
of roses held back behind a fence,
your feet would slide between
cracked oysters and fine grit.
And you would hurry to where
the grass began—window-light
inclining into a studied shadow—
even the prickled leaves less painful
to walk through. On that beach,
you might be reminded of a writer
returning to the page, the pale coastline
like paper, words that seem intimate
with their hurries and hesitations,
they could be damp bodies
approaching awkwardly and unsure.

Domestic Policy

Today I didn't say divorce
    because I was sickened by
            the news
from Afghanistan, translators and their families
        left waiting at the gates,
while American personnel
                lifted off
in the wide indifference of their transport planes.
I said divorce because
    I hadn't made space
          in the cabinet for my husband's things,
and he was angry
            I did not leave
a vacancy for what he carried home from war.
I was tired of him
    stacking bowls
          on the top rack of the dishwasher,
a policy
                I can't abide
when the lower rack is an open country
    waiting to be washed clean.
            Forgive me, reader,
for the weakness
          of my marriage.
I didn't say divorce
    because my husband would rather a drone
            hover above
a wedding procession,
                the party far below,
embroidered dresses glinting, small mirrors sewn into the hems.
He prefers a pilot fire
    from a distant, unendangered screen.
        And I believe
killing should come
            with a risk of dying for the killers.

But that's not why I said divorce.
Forgive me, reader, for the poems
of closets and kitchens.
Marriage is not
two ideologies fighting at a table,
while the soup goes cold
on the spoon.
Marriage is two people
shouting about spices,
the ordering of jars—by alphabet or continent—
as if everything depends
on an ounce of turmeric fading
under glass.
Perhaps, I said divorce
for all the wrong reasons.
Forgive me
for scrubbing the pot with a bristled brush.
My fury
at the gold-stained enamel
is almost the same size as my rage
that somewhere a helicopter
strikes on civilians tonight.
Forgive my sentiment.
All I can do is keep scraping
the dried burning from the pan.

Pledge

Now we are here at home in the little nation
of our marriage, swearing allegiance to the table
we set for lunch or the wind chime on the porch,

its easy dissonance. Even in our shared country,
the afternoon allots its golden lines
so that we're seated, both in shadow, on opposite

ends of a couch and two gray dogs between us.
There are acres of opinions in this house.
I make two cups of tea, two bowls of soup,

divide an apple equally. If I were a patriot,
I would call the blanket we spread across our bed
the only flag—some nights we've burned it

with our anger at each other. Some nights
we've welcomed the weight, a woolen scratch
on both our skins. My love, I am pledging

to this republic, for however long we stand,
I'll watch with you the rain's arrival in our yard.
We'll lift our faces, together, toward the glistening.

Civilian

These days, I'm mostly grateful
   he's one of us, no longer

a piece of metal stamped with
   his name, identifying

facts. He no longer jangles,
   the click of steel to steel, no

more in service to a ship
   or the gray machinery

of the state. Now when we touch,
   I can feel his edge worn down

and barely miss the keenness
   of his mouth. I remember:

for decades he wore two tags
   around his neck, one to leave

with the body, the other,
   perhaps, brought back to my hands.

ACKNOWLEDGMENTS

These poems first appeared in the following publications:

American Life in Poetry: "Pledge"; *Beloit Poetry Journal:* "Brothers"; *Birmingham Poetry Review:* "Pygmalion and Galatea," "Rereading Ovid in Denton, TX," and "As for Penelope—"; *Blackbird:* "My Husband's Father" and "Open Spaces"; *Cincinnati Review:* "As You Were" and "Hail and Farewell"; *Consequence:* "Civilian [There's a ship inside my husband]," "The Veteran in a New Field," and "We Lived in Another Century of War"; *Copper Nickel:* "A War Is Forever"; *The Hudson Review:* "The Acme No. 470 Clicker"; *Los Angeles Review:* "Trench Whistle"; *Narrative Magazine:* "The Trojan Women," "Hyacinthus," "Apologia," and "Philoctetes"; *New England Review:* "What Do You Give the War that Has Everything"; *Nimrod International Journal:* "Metamorphoses"; *Pleiades:* "Civilian [I Bring the War Into My Bed Each Night]"; *Poetry Northwest:* "Flight 2270" and "The Billet"; *Southern Review:* "Norfolk, VA"; *Subtropics:* "Naval Reserve Officer Training Corps"; *Wrath-Bearing Tree:* "Epic War Poem," "Domestic Policy" (published as "Poem for the Reader Who Said My Poems Were Sentimental and Should Engage in a More Complex Moral Reckoning with U.S. Military Actions"), "Some Final Notes on Odysseus," and "Tyrian Purple"; and *Verse Daily:* "As for Penelope" and "Brothers."

"Pledge" was featured on the Poetry Foundation as the Poem of the Day and was included in *How to Love the World: Poems of Gratitude and Hope* (2021), edited by James Crews, and in *More in Time: A Tribute to Ted Kooser,* edited by Marco Abel, Jessica Poli, and Timothy Schaffert (2021).

www.ingramcontent.com/pod-product-compliance
Lightning Source LLC
Chambersburg PA
CBHW021712310125
21207CB00019B/191

* 9 7 8 0 8 0 7 1 8 3 7 2 4 *